Pete Has Fast Feet

Suzanne I. Barchers

Consultants

Robert C. Calfee, Ph.D.
Stanford University

P. David Pearson, Ph.D.
University of California, Berkeley

Publishing Credits

Dona Herweck Rice, *Editor-in-Chief*
Lee Aucoin, *Creative Director*
Sharon Coan, M.S.Ed., *Project Manager*
Jamey Acosta, *Editor*
Robin Erickson, *Designer*
Cathie Lowmiller, *Illustrator*
Robin Demougeot, *Associate Art Director*
Heather Marr, *Copy Editor*
Rachelle Cracchiolo, M.S.Ed., *Publisher*

Teacher Created Materials

5301 Oceanus Drive
Huntington Beach, CA 92649-1030
http://www.tcmpub.com

ISBN 978-1-4333-2915-9

Meet Pete. He has fast feet.

If Dad has a need,
Pete will help at top
speed.

Dad can rake or
weed. Pete will do
a good deed.

Pete runs fast to greet his pals on Main Street.

With fast feet and knees, he is fast as the breeze.

Pete can race to the creek any day of the week.

Pete can race to the
tree. He can race a
fast bee!

A hill may be steep.
Pete is as fast as a
jeep.

Beep, beep! Clear the street! Beep, beep! There goes Pete.

In rain or in sleet,
Pete is fast on his
feet.

From his toes to each heel, he is strong like steel.

He may not make a peep, but Pete runs in his sleep!

Decodable Words

and	Dad	hill	need	sleet
as	day	his	not	speed
at	deed	if	on	steel
be	fast	in	pals	steep
bee	feet	jeep	peep	Street
beep	goes	knees	Pete	toes
breeze	greet	like	race	top
but	has	Main	rain	tree
can	he	make	rake	weed
clear	heel	may	runs	week
creek	help	meet	sleep	will

Sight Words

a	good	there
any	is	to
are	of	with
do	or	
from	the	

Challenge Word
each

Extension Activities

Discussion Questions

- How does Pete help his dad? (*He carries the leaves.*)

- What is Pete dreaming about? (*He dreams about winning a race.*)

- Do you think Pete runs because he is late like his sister Kate or because he just likes to run? Why?

Exploring the Story

- Discuss the words *deed*, *feet*, and *need*. Write them so you can see how they are spelled. Ask children to find other words in the story with the same pattern (*beep*, *heel*, *jeep*, *meet*, *peep*, *weed*, and *week*). Discuss how the combination *ee* makes the long vowel sound heard at the beginning of the word *eel*.

- Which words have the same pattern but also begin with a blend of two consonants, such as *speed*? (*creek*, *greet*, *sleep*, *steel*, *steep*, and *street*)

- Write the words *beep*, *deed*, *feet*, *heel*, *jeep*, *meet*, *need*, *peep*, *weed*, and *week* on small sheets of paper. Place the papers facedown in a large circle on the floor or outside. For one player: Have him or her start at the paper with the word *feet* written on it, read the word aloud, run to the next card, pick it up, and read the word aloud before running to the next word. Continue until the circle is completed. Mix the cards up and repeat. For two or more players, create more circles or have players take turns. For a challenge, add the words *creek*, *greet*, *sleep*, *speed*, *steel*, *steep*, and *street*. Vary the game by hopping, galloping, or skipping to the cards.